The Monstructor

Written by Joanna Rowland
Illustrations by Melissa Goodman

The Monstructor
Text Copyright © 2017 by Joanna Rowland
Artwork Copyright © 2017 by Melissa Goodman

Summary: Naughty Monsters. Have they forgot? To learn their
manners they must be taught. Little monsters are acting like humans
at school. Oh no! Their teacher gets the Monstructor to come in a
save the day.

Clear Fork Publishing
P.O. Box 870
102 S. Swenson
Stamford, Texas 79553
(325)773-5550
www.clearforkpublishing.com

Printed and Bound in the United States of America.
ISBN - 978-1-946101-43-3
LCN - 2017952988

www.clearforkpublishing.com

"To Ari and Ian. My two little monsters, the Monstructor would give you both an A+." - Melissa

To Mrs. Rowland's students. You make teaching so much fun and inspire me every day. - Joanna

'Twas one stormy night
when the Monstructor flew
to the school to teach monsters
a manner or two.

She flew in the class
with a boo and a hiss
and told little monsters
"Now, listen to this."

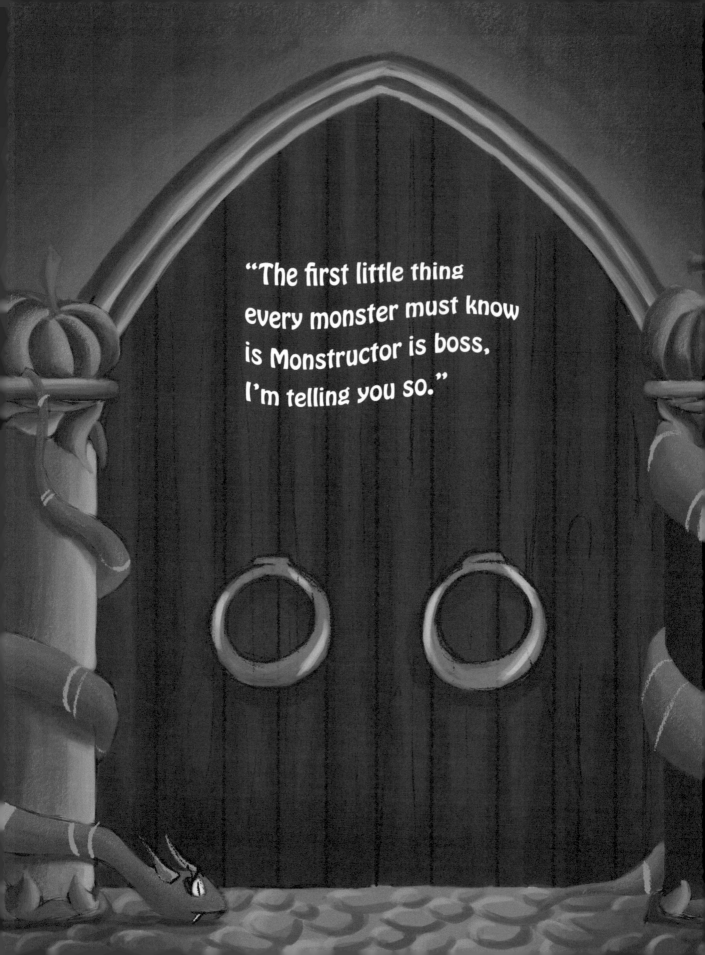

"The first little thing
every monster must know
is Monstructor is boss,
I'm telling you so."

"I heard from your teacher
that this class forgot
how school monsters act
so by me you'll be taught."

"At night time when school starts
arrive with your ooze,
ready to recite
your grrs and your boos."

At story time they sat
so still on the floor.
The Monstructor asked shocked,
"Where's your rolling and roar?"

"Float to the ceiling,
never sit at your desk!
Just like good monsters do
when they want to impress."

The monsters wrote neatly,
the Monstructor screeched!
"You are not children.
Write messy," she preached.

She taught them to drip
snotty ink from their nose
for writing instead of
with fingers or toes.

"We monsters don't wait.
That's what human kids do.
We're sloppy, and messy
and covered with goo."

The monsters listened closely
and their eyes grew so wide.
They booed and they hissed
in true monster pride.

"We're ready to learn,"
said the monsters at school.
"Just give us a chance.
We don't need one more rule."

And then just like that
the little monsters got smart,
splashing paint on each other
for their monster art.

The class dripped with messes
from ceiling to floor.
With roars and disruptions,
the Monstructor yelled, "More!"

The class was chaotic -
no order at all!
The Monstructor smirked
at monsters having a ball!

As their teacher came back,
the Monstructor flew,
happy those monsters
had learned a manner or two.

Joanna Rowland writes picture books for children. She likes to write about subjects that tug at her heart and silly stories. She is the author of Always Mom, Forever Dad and The Memory Box. She is a member of the Society Of Children's Writers and Illustrators. Joanna grew up in Sacramento, CA where she still lives with her husband and three daughters. She's a kindergarten teacher, a synchronized swimming coach, and writer but her favorite job is being a mom.
Check out her website at www.writerrowland.com.

Melissa Goodman loves to draw. She has a bachelor's degree in illustration. When she is not drawing, she's busy raising her 2 young sons. She lives in Washington State with her family, where the beautiful landscape around her continues to inspire her work.
Check out her website at melissagoodman.artstation.com

CPSIA information can be obtained
at www.ICGtesting.com
Printed in the USA
LVHW072129290720
661905LV00012B/190